A Visit to the Butterfly House

By Annette Smith
Illustrations by Sarah Davis

On Saturday morning,
my big sister, Lee, took me
to the butterfly house.
It was in the town gardens.

This was the first time
we had been to the butterfly house.
I was very happy
because I love butterflies.

A man from the butterfly house held the door open for us.

I got a surprise as we moved inside because the air was so hot. Lee told me that butterflies don't like to be cold.

First, the man showed us a **card**.
It had photos of all the butterflies
we would see in the butterfly house.

Some of the butterflies were blue.
Some were white and some were green.

One butterfly had big red spots
on its wings.

The butterfly house
looked like a big, green garden.
It was much bigger
than our garden at home.

We saw plants
with big leaves all around them.

I saw a plant that had bananas
growing on a long **stem**.

As we came slowly past a little **pool,**
some butterflies flew away.
They went up to the top
of the butterfly house.

But lots of butterflies
didn't fly away from us.

They just stayed on the leaves
of the plants.
We could see the lines and spots
on their wings.

Then, a beautiful blue butterfly
flew down onto my hand.
I sat very still
because I didn't want to scare it.

Lee took a photo
of the butterfly on my hand.

I was sad when it opened its wings
and flew away.

Lee gave me the camera
so that I could take some photos.

A little boy and his grandma
came over to watch us.
The little boy laughed when a butterfly
sat on Lee's head.

We had a very good time today.
We liked all the butterflies.
But the blue one was my favourite.

Glossary

card thick paper

pool a small pond of water

stem the branch from the plant to the fruit